James Howard Kunstler

The Fall of
the Ancients

A Tale of Fortitude
and Triumph

———————————

ALSO BY JAMES HOWARD KUNSTLER

Fiction

A Safe and Happy Place

The World Made By Hand Series
The Harrows of Spring
A History of the Future
The Witch of Hebron
World Made By Hand

Maggie Darling, a Modern Romance
Thunder Island
The Halloween Ball
The Hunt
Blood Solstice
An Embarrassment of Riches
The Life of Byron Jaynes
A Clown in the Moonlight
The Wampanaki Tales.

Nonfiction

Too Much Magic
The Long Emergency
The City in Mind
Home From Nowhere
The Geography of Nowhere

James Howard Kunstler

The Fall of
the Ancients

A Tale of Fortitude
and Triumph

A Novella

The Greenaway Series
Book Six

Highbrow Press

Published in the United States of America

ISBN 9781723868108

Highbrow Press
PO Box 193
Saratoga Springs
New York, 12866

Ponsonby Hall, a heap of red sandstone in the imposing Richardsonian Romanesque style, all turrets, arches and pointy finials, with a ponderous rusticated gray granite base, came into view among the pines and birches as the Greenaway family — Robert, Evelyn and son Jeffrey — swung up the great curving driveway in their rented Chevrolet. The family had driven 279 miles from Manhattan to the wilds of New Hampshire that September day of the year 1963 to deposit Jeff in a boarding school for boys deemed to be "thriving indifferently," as the advertisement in the back pages of *The Times Sunday Magazine* put it.

The Greenaway boy had behaved not just badly but quite spectacularly badly in the year arcing toward his upcoming twelfth birthday. He'd run away from home two days before Christmas. He'd gone amok at a penthouse birthday party for a classmate enemy and destroyed a lot of personal property (the boy's presents, the cake). He'd taken to sneaking out of the apartment on East 79th Street late at night to consort at the Channel Five TV studio with the nut-case known as Count Zackuloff, who hosted the midnight horror movie. And there was the matter of his recently concluded season at the suddenly defunct Camp Timahoe — not Jeff's fault, really, but another ominous thread of misadventure in a childhood career that had come to seem oddly accursed.

Being Return Day, the campus was thronged with other parents depositing their offspring for the fall term. The Greenaways parked in a space just vacated by a Cadillac the size of a ferryboat. A little way ahead, a maroon English Bentley motorcar pulled into the yawning porte-cochère. A door opened and a red-headed boy came tumbling out, shoved by a gray trouser leg that terminated in a black wingtip shoe. Seconds later, a leather suitcase flew out, knocking the boy down again just as he'd pulled himself to his knees. Then the fine car sped off. The boy, seventeen and in the Sixth Form (or Grade 12), dusted himself off and disappeared with his bag inside the Great Hall, as the building was called.

The Greenaway parents goggled at this scene with a certain speechless dismay, roiled as they were with very mixed feelings about their decision to enroll Jeff in a place renowned for straightening out willful, insolent, and obdurate boys.

"You're not going to do that to me, are you?" Jeff asked, not a little in jest.

"Oh, Pussycat, really," his mother said, a lump in her throat.

"I wonder what he did to deserve that?" Jeff's father mumbled.

Jeff had mixed feelings about being yanked out of his familiar haunts in New York City, away from his friends, and installed in a remote sleep-away school for hard cases. But the previous year had been his last in the elementary grades, and his gang of friends was breaking up anyway, each kid sent to a different private school, so he'd see less of them from now on. And he was favorably impressed so far with Ponsonby Hall's spooky trappings, which resembled the headquarters of various fiends played by Vincent Price in the horror movies. He liked the closeness of the seemingly endless woods, too, nature being in short supply back home in Manhattan. He was even a little thrilled at the prospect of living in a community of "screw-ups" like himself, kids who had at least done something interesting in life.

"Well, let's hunt down Dr. Stilgoe," Jeff's father said, stepping out into the strong mountain sunshine.

Harry Raymond Stilgoe, PhD, had been headmaster of Ponsonby Hall since the early years of World War Two, taking over from the school's beloved founder, Dr. Cecil Hatch, who died at age eighty-three in a freak Christmas vacation accident when he encountered a swarm of stinging sea nettles in the surf off Jekyll Island, Georgia. His successor, H.R. "Doc" Stilgoe had already garnered some renown in his own right as the author of over a score of books about woodcraft and Indian Lore, most notably *A Boy's*

Book of the Savage Nations and Their Ways (Bobbs-Merrill, 1937). Doc Stilgoe's own sterling character was forged when, upon his twenty-first birthday, his father Ivor Stilgoe, professor of scientific business management at Cornell University, presented the young man with an itemized invoice for all the expenses connected with his upbringing, including the fee charged by the doctor who delivered him. It was not a joke. He paid the bill, but never spoke to his father again. Nor, according to his entry in *Who's Who*, had the great man ever married, having dedicated himself to rescuing the errant children of others.

They found him on the terrace on the back side of the Great Hall, circulating magnetically among the returning boys and their parents. A table of welcoming refreshments was laid: lemonade and sugar cookies, made by Mrs. Dinsmoor, the school cook. The headmaster stood but five-foot-five — some of the older boys loomed over him — but moved panther-like with athletic muscularity that came from his near-religious adherence to the Royal Canadian Air Force daily calisthenics regimen, which the boys, too, were required to perform every morning after chapel and before breakfast. His ruddy face was ornamented by an old-fashioned "soup-strainer" mustache. In his beloved expeditionary khakis and pith helmet he looked a bit like his own childhood hero, Theodore Roosevelt. "Doc" had set up a telescope on the terrace for the occasion to emphasize Ponsonby Hall's dedication to science. The lens was trained on the summit of distant Mount Cardigan, where the resident ranger was expected to climb the stairs to his fire tower with a week's groceries. It was said that one could set a clock by the ranger's comings and goings.

"Ah, and you must be young Greenaway, one of the new boys," Stilgoe said, seizing Jeff's hand and pumping it manfully. The headmaster recognized Jeff's father and mother from the meeting they'd had at the Drake Hotel in New York back in June, when the arrangements were made. "What a fine young fellow! You're in two-west-twenty-two. That's the second floor, west wing, room twenty-two, bunking with Hohenhorst, Arthur." The headmaster was reputed to have a prodigious memory for the smallest details and that little about the complex doings at the school escaped his attention. In fact, it served his purposes for the boys to think he was omniscient and omnipresent. "Good to have you aboard—"

"There he is!" cried 14-year-old Howie Shanks from the telescope, meaning the returning ranger. The day after his parents' divorce was finalized, the freckled third former had stolen a car from a neighbor in Nutley, New Jersey, and driven halfway to Pittsburgh before the state police corralled him at a gas station outside

Hublersburg. It was the Judge who suggested Ponsonby Hall.

"Hey, he's got a girl with him!" Shanks cried. "Boy, is she built!"

"Move aside, son!" Stilgoe barked and leaned into the eyepiece. "Hmmm," he said, adjusting the focus. "The Forest Service will hear about this!" He stuck the lens caps on each end of the instrument and folded its tripod legs. Below the terrace, a gang of older boys played touch football in golden sunlight on an exquisitely groomed athletic field. Many parents had drifted back to their cars. A hint of the fall color to come blazed in the crimson sumacs and Virginia creeper at the margin of the dark woods.

"I think I'm going to like it here," Jeff said to no one in particular.

*

Following the final farewells to parents at half-past four, the boys were all sent to their rooms to "settle in" before supper. There, Jeff encountered his new room-mate, Arthur Hohenhorst, a pale, diminutive child with facial features so indistinct that he resembled a more primitive creature, say, a shipworm. He sat in the center of his bed with his knees drawn up protectively to his chest and his arms around his knees.

Jeff introduced himself and extended his hand. Arthur's damp hand was positively slimy.

"What are you here for?" Jeff asked.

"School," Arthur said.

"We're all here for that," Jeff said. "What'd you do to get sent here?"

"Nothing."

"It must have been something."

"They said I set the house on fire."

"Jeez, did you?"

"I dunno...."

Arthur's eyes seemed fixed on some indeterminate middle distance.

"How could you not know?"

Arthur shrugged his shoulders.

"Do me a favor," Jeff said. "Try not to burn this place down while I'm here."

The room smelled of fresh paint. Each boy had a small desk, a narrow bed, half of a closet, and a chest of drawers. In his top draw Jeff found a graffiti that said *Die Jew scum*. He imagined it was left by some Nazi sympathizer during the war years. Had the Nazis won the war, there wouldn't be any Sandy Koufax, he reflected. Lost in these puzzles of history, Jeff unpacked his suitcase, hung his two extra pairs of khakis in the closet, and tested his bed. The springs were weak and the mattress slumped into a valley that seemed to match Jeff's slumping spirits. Arthur hadn't uttered another word in the meantime.

"Want to know what I did to get sent here?" Jeff asked.

"Okay, what?"

"I robbed a bank."

"How come you're not in reform school?"

"Isn't that what this is?" Jeff said.

"Oh… yeah…well… I guess," Arthur said.

Just then, the door burst open and two older boys entered the room. One was the red-haired boy so rudely expelled from the Bentley limousine earlier, Edgar Uhle, known as "Frosty," from Darien, Connecticut. He held the current record for most schools expelled from prior to Ponsonby Hall: six, including the Nygungu Academy in Kenya — his father was posted there for a year by the State Department — a most severe institution in the Rift Valley, where boys, mostly former British colonials, were subject to caning and thrashing by the masters. Frosty had tried running away along an old railroad track, only to discover that there was nothing out there between himself and the entire wild kingdom of the African veldt. The great herds were visible clear out to the horizon. Then he spotted a pack of hyenas in a nearby dry-wash feeding on a three-day old gnu carcass, and sprinted the half-mile back to the school screeching his lungs raw. Of course, he was caned for being absent at the noon meal.

The other older boy was Russell Shane, darkly handsome with slicked back hair, caramel-colored tortoiseshell eyeglasses, and taped up penny loafers. "Shaner," as he was called, had sunk the family yacht off Fisher's Island, two summers ago in a freak accident involving a spear gun and a propane tank.

"Welcome maggots," Frosty said. "Having fun yet?"

Jeff didn't know how to answer. Arthur remained mute.

"I'm speaking to you, zygote," Frosty said.

"Just settling in, like they told us to," Jeff replied.

"Oh?" Shaner said. "A wise guy?"

"Not wising off," Jeff said, "Unpacking, is all."

"Do you know who we are?"

"You're... older guys."

"Yes we are. We're the Ancients," Frosty said. "We run the place."

Arthur began mewling.

"Awwww," Shaner said. "What's widdle Twinkie upset about? Homesick alweady?"

"Leave me alone," Arthur whined.

Shaner fairly leaped upon the boy, pinned Arthur's arms to the mattress with his knees and administered a series of noogies about the younger boy's skull.

"Get offa him!" Jeff cried.

Next thing he knew, Frosty was atop him, applying noogies similarly.

"Rule number one," Frosty said. "Never talk back to an Ancient."

"Rule number two," Shaner said from atop Arthur. "Never rat on an Ancient."

"Rule number three," Frosty said. "Always do what we say."

Frosty and Shaner climbed off and made as if to dust off their shirts.

"Tonight's a special night," Frosty said. "Count Furfur requests your presence in the old stable. It's the annual initiation."

"Count Furfur?"

"The Duke of Earl of Hell," Shaner explained.

"Rule number four," Frosty said. "Maggots never utter the name Count Furfur. He is to be addressed only as *him*. Just do what you're told. Be there. The old stable. At nine o'clock."

"Isn't lights out at nine o'clock?" Jeff said.

"For maggots maybe," Frosty said with a snort. "Ancients never sleep."

Shaner giggled.

"Where is it, this old stable?"

"Follow the primrose path. You'll see a red light there. Don't be late."

"Rule number five," Shaner said. "Don't talk about initiation. See you later. Or else."

*

Supper — the mysterious chipped creamed beef on toast with peas — was a glum affair among the new arrivals, the boys of the first form, the equivalent of seventh grade back in the normal world. That lost world suddenly seemed as hopelessly remote as Never Never Land. The table of the Two-West boys, all fourteen of them, was presided over by the Master of Two West, one Khan Hamdoon, who doubled as a teacher of literature and rhetoric. Hamdoon, at 39, had a double-chin so pronounced it might have been mistaken for a goiter, and a dramatic British military-style mustache with waxed and pointed ends that extended a full two inches beyond his cheeks. He had come to New York after the war on a special visa for Indian army veterans who had fought alongside the Yanks against the Japanese in Burma. The city had horrified him in its scale and commotion, and he felt so fortunate to find a position at Ponsonby Hall that he'd barely left his refuge since arriving, except for a yearly trip accompanying headmaster Stilgoe to the Peabody Museum at Harvard. Hamdoon was wounded in the siege of Meiktila near Mandlay in '45, losing his left hand at the wrist. He had become remarkably adept since then at using the slightly V-shaped wrist stump in the tasks of everyday life. Jeff, sitting just to the Master's right, was so disturbed at the sight of Hamdoon gripping the knife handle in those flipper-like flanges, that he couldn't eat.

"Vat is the matter with you, boy," Hamdoon asked Jeff in his musical dialect. "You must take nutrition or you vill vither away and then vee vill have to bury you in the special cemetery for boys who starved themselves to death, heh heh heh."

"I can't figure out what this stuff is," Jeff said. He was old enough to know that it would have been unkind to admit that Hamdoon's stump disgusted him.

"This is the lovely chippity beef. Specialty of the maison! Veddy veddy delicious. If you vill not eat yours, pass it this vay and I vill show you a magic trick, heh heh heh."

Jeff pushed the plate in Hamdoon's direction. The master gobbled it up inside five seconds and shoved the plate back in front of Jeff.

"See? Magic! Chippity beef vanishes! How do you think this happened?"

"You ate it," Jeff said.

"No, no, no, no, no. You did not see me eat this."

"Of course I did."

"Silly boy," Hamdoon said. "All first form boys are silly. You vill learn, heh heh heh."

*

Just after nine o'clock, Jeff left the sleeping Arthur behind in Two-West-Twenty-two, an inert lump under his blankets with a tiny blow-hole for air. The halls and stairwell of the Great Hall resounded with stony silence as Jeff padded down them. From the back terrace on the ground floor, he could discern a red light not a great distance away. He hurried alone across the playing field toward it under a horrifying canopy of stars, any one of which, he worried, might actually be the spacecraft of malicious extraterrestrials bent on exterminating mankind. As he approached the fine old stable building in its piney grove, he could hear rock and roll music playing, and saw flickering candlelight in a set of three dormers. The exterior lamp with its red bulb hung above the open carriage door. The song playing was "The Monkey Time" by Major Lance. He entered the building.

"You're late, maggot," a deep voice intoned as Jeff emerged up the stairs into the spacious loft from which the music emanated. All heads turned to him: the sixteen other new boys of the first form (not including Arthur) seated on benches as in a crude woodland chapel, and the three Ancients at the far end — that is, Shaner and Frosty seated at either side of someone caparisoned in a remarkably life-like paper-mache deer-head mask, antlers and all, attached to a red satin cape. This central figure presided on a kind of crude throne, actually a 19th century armchair spray-painted gold. In his right hand he gripped a stage espontoon, a sort of pike with a rubber spear point, last used in a 1959 school production of *Julius Caesar* by the Bard of Avon.

"What's your explanation, maggot?" Shaner barked.

All the other boys had turned to goggle at Jeff.

Jeff shrugged.

"Let's get this straight," a resonant voice inside the deer-head intoned, "You turn up late at the most important night of your life?"

"I don't even know what this is about."

"It's where we decide whether you live or die," Frosty said.

"Where's your room-mate?" Shaner snarled, hoisting a clipboard up to the candlelight and squinting at it. "Hohenhorst, Arthur."

"Asleep back in the room."

"And you didn't wake him up?"

"I'm not his keeper."

"You are from now on," Frosty said. "Make sure that he comes whenever we summon this bunch of maggots...."

"Or we give you the business," Shaner added. "Now siddown!"

"The Monkey Time" ended and another 45 rpm record dropped on the portable phonograph: "Duke of Earl," by Gene Chandler.

The deer-headed figure began tapping the butt-end of his pike on the plank floor in time with the song. His cohorts chanted along with introductory lyrics:

Duke, Duke, Duke, Duke of Earl
Duke, Duke, Duke of Earl...

Halfway through the number, the deer-headed figure at center lifted off the bulky mask and dumped it behind his throne.

"That's enough of that crap," he said. "Kill the music!"

Frosty obliged, not without scraping the needle across the disk, making a painful noise like fingernails on a blackboard.

"Smoke! Light!" the boy at center cried. Shaner knocked a Marlboro out of a pack for him and Frosty lit a match. The boy at center took a deep drag and exhaled a train of smoke rings, as if demonstrating the pleasures of tobacco to a TV audience. "The pause that refreshes," he remarked. "Permit me to introduce myself: Jack C. Hannon. The C is for can't-believe-you-maggots. You can just call me Hannon. I run this outfit. No, not this little kaffeeklatsch here. The school. That's right. The whole shootin' match. I let people like your maggoty parents believe that Doc Stilgoe runs the show. It ain't so. How did I arrive at this exalted position? By dedication to my cause and, frankly, dogged hard work. Beverage!" He clapped his hands.

Frosty hefted a thermos bottle, and poured a clear liquid into a martini glass. Hannon took a big sip. He was surprisingly pale and thin, almost cadaverous, with flops of golden hair symmetrically arrayed on each side of the part. His nose was very complicated — a blade with bumps and indentations. His voice had a reptilian quality of insinuation, whatever he actually said. Most of all he had the peculiar quality of looking at once youthful and very old, To Jeff, he resembled one of the undead from the horror movie mill of Hammer Films.

"Ah…. That's better," Hannon said. "Okay, here's the deal, maggots: you're here in the service of The Ancients now. In exchange, you get protection from anything, uh, untoward happening to you or your stuff. It's like insurance. You pay five bucks a month, which, frankly, you must agree is a reasonable sum, considering. I know your maggot parents are gonna send you at least that much and, let's face it, there's nowhere to spend it around here, anyway. At least nowhere for maggots. If we call on any of you for a shoeshine or to make a bed or take out the garbage, you will snap to your duty. If you fail to answer any summons, there will be consequences."

Hannon stepped off his throne and strolled by the new boys on their benches, pausing before each one.

"What'd you do, maggot?" he asked one with a strawberry-colored birthmark that ran from his neck nearly up to his cheekbone.

"Do…?"

"To get sent to Ponsey Prep?"

"Oh. I dunno."

"You don't know? Hell, I know what I did."

"Whadja do?" Shaner and Frosty barked in unison.

"Me?" Hannon said, theatrically. "Why, I shot a man in Reno, just to watch him die." He took a sip of his cocktail. There was an audible gasp from the younger boys. "So, what was your dastardly deed, maggot?"

"I punched my sister," the boy admitted.

Hannon carefully switched hands with his cocktail and punched the boy directly in the solar plexus without spilling a drop. The target went down squealing and wheezing.

"Don't ever punch a girl again," Hannon said, stepping over him. "It's ungentlemanly. How about you, little white worm?" he asked the next boy in line.

"Talked back," the boy answered.

"Your folks get sick of it?"

"Apparently."

"You wouldn't talk back to me? Would you?"

Hannon grabbed his ear and twisted it. The boy curled sideways in pain.

"No!" he cried. "I worship you!"

"I like this one," Hannon said to his colleagues. "What's your name?"

"Albert Peavy."

"You can shine my shoes, Albert."

And so it went down the line. Fighting in school. Poor grades. Truancy. Bad attitude. Caught shoplifting. Blowing things up with cherry bombs. Soon, Hannon came to Jeff at the end of the bench.

"Speak maggot."

"I robbed a bank," Jeff said.

All three Ancients burst out laughing. In the process, Hannon sprayed gin all over Jeff's face.

"Really? That's rich. Which bank?"

"Chase Manhattan."

"What! You robbed my father's bank?"

"I didn't know you then."

"You don't know me now," Hannon said grinning. "The real me. What'd you do with the money?"

"I spent it all on a girl," Jeff said.

The other boys started whispering among themselves."

"You're a doozy," Hannon said. "But don't imagine you're in for special treatment. There was a kid here once who said he killed his mother and got away with it. He was liar. Are you a liar, Maggot?"

"No."

"How come you're not in Sing Sing."

"My father's an attorney."

"Oh? He get you off?"

"Yeah, he pleaded insanity."

Hannon took a step away from Jeff and knocked back the remainder of his cocktail.

"How come you're not in the insane asylum."

"They said this place was worse," Jeff said.

Hannon guffawed and put a headlock on Jeff, who tried to wriggle out of his grasp but couldn't, and applied several noogies to Jeff's skull.

"You may end up being my pet maggot," Hannon said. "In which case, there is something special you can do for me." He let go of Jeff, pulled down his khaki pants and boxers, turned around, and presented his bare bottom. "Kiss it!" he said.

"I'm not gonna do that," Jeff said.

"You're a hard case. I'm afraid we're gonna have to crack you."

Hannon hiked his pants back up and instructed the rest of the boys to form two lines. Frosty and Shaner took Jeff by each arm and dragged him to the opening of the gantlet of boys. Hannon, at the far end, explained the procedure. Jeff was thrust within where he was kicked, pummeled, smacked, and stomped. At the end, he lay curled in a ball, like an armadillo. Shaner and Frosty added a few last kicks.

"Welcome to Ponsonby Hall, maggots," Hannon said, and the three Ancients hurriedly left the loft chanting "Duke, Duke, Duke, Duke of Earl, Duke Duke..." until the new boys of first form were left alone there.

Two of them helped Jeff off the floor and dusted him off like a rag doll that had been dragged around by the family dog.

"Hey, we're sorry about that," said Andrew Veach of Saddle River, New Jersey, a chronic malingerer.

"Yeah, they made us do it," added Eldon Andelthorne, Veach's room-mate, a near-albino from Hartford, who wounded the neighbor's cat with an air rifle.

Jeff limped back to the Great Hall with them, and up to their room (Two-West-Seventeen) with several other of the first formers, where they became better acquainted, bragged, complained, and essayed to assess their situation until well after midnight.

*

And so the fall term launched, and routines established, and classes commenced, and the days rushed by, and the foliage in the New Hampshire hills caught fire, and the nights grew chilly, and the boys of the first form attended Hannon and the Ancients in the scant free hours when they were not scheduled, or eating, or made to run across the playing fields after balls of various sizes and shapes.

Jeff was not ordained as a "pet," exactly, but found himself appointed as "valet" to the Ancients. He was taught by Shaner how to iron an oxford shirt and was required to prepare fresh ones daily for the three overlords. In the idle hour before supper each evening, when other boys studied or wrote letters home, he was assigned to make and serve cocktails to the Ancients who lounged around the luxurious fifth floor tower suite they occupied — said to have been Doc Stilgoe's quarters until Hannon evicted him — along with some other favored members of the sixth form. (Jeff became adept at mixing martinis, manhattans, vodka stingers, and side-cars.) One Saturday night, while the rest of the students watched a movie in the rec hall (*Wee Geordie* with Alastair Sim), the Ancients held a party in their suite, to which were invited several young women from the nearby mill town of Orcus, one of which Hannon referred to as his "fiancé." As far as Jeff could ascertain, these "ladies" were somewhat beyond high school age, and affected a slatternly mode of dress, and he saw one or another accept a wad of cash.

Jeff was smacked occasionally for "dilly-dallying," or spilling gin on someone's pants, or dropping a tray, but he carried out his duties and did what he could to avoid being persecuted. Other boys were not so fortunate. Arthur Hohenhorst, for instance. The night after the initiation ceremony, as Jeff puzzled over the chapter in his math textbook titled *Introduction to Elementary Equations*, Hannon's two henchmen turned up in room Two-West-twenty-two and spirited the terrified child away. An hour later, Arthur was returned by Frosty and Shaner like a duffle bag heaved into a storage closet. Jeff could see that he was covered with bleeding scratches, as if he had been dragged through a bramble thicket — which is more or less what Arthur had been subjected to, along with other humiliations. When the two persecutors left, Jeff rushed to help Arthur off the floor.

"What'd they do to you?" he asked.

"Nothing," Arthur said.

"Obviously that's not true."

"Leave me alone."

"Want me to get Doc Stilgoe?"

"No," Arthur said and, once he was on his feet, shook Jeff off.

"How about Mr. Hamdoon?"

"Just leave me alone," Arthur said and limped to his bed, where he went inert. Minutes later, the PA system in the hallway announced lights out, as usual playing a lush orchestral arrangement of Brahm's Lullaby (Op. 49, No. 4).

Hours later, Jeff woke in the dark to the sound of Arthur whimpering on the other side of the room.

"Are you okay?" Jeff whispered.

Arthur refused to answer.

The next morning, after chapel and before breakfast, when there was a good deal of milling around in the hallway outside the refectory, Jeff did indeed seek out the Master of the first form's lodgings on Two-West, Khan Hamdoon.

"Some older kids are beating up on my room-mate," Jeff said, eyes darting as he warily tried to spot the Ancients in the crowd.

"Nothing to vorry about," Hamdoon said. "Boy stuff. Same as ever was."

"No, you don't understand. They really hurt him."

"Of course they did," Hamdoon said. "It vouldn't be real boy stuff if it didn't hurt."

"But he didn't do anything."

"He must have done something. This is not done for no reason."

"He's just a pathetic kid," Jeff said. "The kind that gets picked on."

"Vell, you see, you have just explained this beautifully!" Hamdoon said, and touseled Jeff's hair with his good hand before striding away in his stiff military gait, going, "heh heh heh... boys boys boys...."

Later that afternoon, Jeff was on the junior athletic field being instructed in elementary handling of the lacrosse stick by assistant coach Ernie Nighthorse, a full-blooded Pennacook Indian, when a great commotion of sirens and clanging bells interrupted the lesson. The boys on the field all turned as one to see the cherry-red trucks of the Orcus fire brigade race up the drive to the Great Hall. A ribbon of smoke curled out of a window on the second floor. Jeff did not deduce that the window in question was that of room Two-West-twenty-two, but he learned as much a little later when the firemen had concluded their business and boarded the hook and ladder for the journey back to the station house.

"You vill be moved to other quarters," Khan Hamdoon informed Jeff as they both peered into the charred and stinking room twenty-two. Arthur's half of the room had sustained the brunt of the damage . It appeared that the bed had been set on fire.

"Where's Arthur?"

"He is no longer here."

"Is he dead?"

"No no no no no," Hamdoon said, wagging his head with its permanent demi-smile of elevated amusement. "Not dead. Perhaps a bit... unbalanced. But he is gone now and it is all for the better."

"I told you he was being picked on."

Hamdoon ignored the remark. "Your clothings and other chattels have been rescued and transferred to Two-West-twenty-seven, with Mr. Knudsen."

Axel Knudsen of Pound Ridge, New York, nicknamed "Stench," was so disregardful of his personal hygiene, despite being required to shower daily, that he had already been through two other room-mates in three weeks. His shoes alone had an odoriferous presence like unto the wild forest swine of the ancient Teutonic folk-tales. An obsessive collector of baseball statistics, Axel's personality type would be popularly known in years to come as Aspergers. His statistical obsessions left little of his attention for regular schoolwork, or anything else for that matter.

"There was a fire in my room," Jeff explained as he sat on his new bed. Axel glanced up from a chart he was compiling of Yankee left-hander Whitey Ford's strikeouts vis-à-vis the temperature and humidity on the days of each start. "They took Arthur away somewhere," Jeff added.

Displaying a mask of perplexity, and not a shred of interest in the fire or the fate of Arthur Hohenhorst, Axel returned to his chart without comment. In a little while, Mr. Hamdoon came by with Pete the janitor to deposit Jeff's things. The aroma of smoke which clung to them was an antidote to the rich miasma of odors wafting from Axel's side of the room.

*

Jeff was not without personal resources, of course, and that very evening, instead of slogging through another fifty pages of the excruciating *Wuthering Heights*, he composed a long letter to his mother and father detailing the tyranny of the Ancients and other irregularities in the Ponsonby Hall scheme of things, concluding with a plea to be allowed to return to New York City and "any other kind of normal school there."

The following afternoon before supper, as October's early darkness slammed over the landscape like a fallen curtain, he was attending to his duties in the Ancients' tower suite when

25

Hannon emerged from a bedroom in his customary green velvet smoking jacket. Jeff did not have to be asked to prepare Hannon's martini. A lugubrious pop song called "The End of the World" sung by one Skeeter Davis was playing on the radio, broadcast by the almighty WBZ out of Boston. Shaner and Frosty soon drifted in. Jeff served them their cocktails and returned to his ironing. He was lost in his own thoughts — of a girl back home with budding breasts he had developed a crush on the previous spring — when he apprehended that Hannon was reading something out loud that sounded familiar. He quickly recognized that it was his own letter home of vilification and complaint. He lifted his head from the ironing board as his internal organs shifted this way and that.

"Ah," Hannon said. "We have your attention."

"Huh...?" Jeff said.

"We review the outgoing mail from time to time, you know."

"Why do you do that?"

"Silly maggot," Hannon cackled. "Did you write this?" He held the letter in two pinched fingers as if it were a pair of soiled underpants.

"I dunno."

"It's addressed to a Mr. and Mrs. Robert Greenaway," Hannon said, now holding up in his other hand the envelope which had been carefully steamed open. "And signed, 'your son, Jeff.' That'd be you, right?"

"I dunno."

"Is there another Greenaway here at Ponsey?"

"I dunno."

"Oh, come on now. We know you're not a moron. Quit acting like one."

"Something's burning," Shaner said.

Jeff seized the iron which had, unfortunately, left a blackish triangular brand across the front placket of one of Frosty's shirts, a pink Brooks Brothers button-down roll-collar oxford.

"Look what he's done!" Frosty said, crossing the room and hoisting the smoldering garment.

"I didn't mean it!"

"Mean it?" Frosty said. "It doesn't matter if you meant it or not. You *did* it. Do you know how hard my father has to work to buy one of these?"

"Your father doesn't work," Shaner said, tittering.

"Well, if he did work," Frosty said. "For instance, if he drove a garbage truck or shucked clams."

"He'd have to shuck about ten thousand clams," Hannon estimated. "Terrible work. I've watched them do it at the yacht club in Boothbay Harbor. Swarthy little men in rubber pants hunched over tin tubs with scarred, stumpy fingers, bleeding from the never-ending drudgery."

"Thank goodness he only has to clip coupons," Frosty said.

Jeff was not really following the badinage.

"We digress," Hannon said. "How dare you try to rat on us."

"Look at him," Shaner said. "Those little rat eyes, little rat paws."

"Little rat thoughts in his little rat skull," Frosty said.

"You're going to write a new and improved letter," Hannon said. "Get over here."

When Jeff came close, Hannon seized his ear and twisted it, guiding him down into the swivel chair at a magnificent carved mahogany desk. He took a sheet of cream-colored laid stationary with the Ponsonby Hall crest out of the top drawer and a ballpoint pen and flung it on the green baize surface.

"Ow!" Jeff cried. "You're ripping my ear off."

"Shut up and take this down. *My dearest Mummy and Dad. There is no place I'd rather be than dear old Ponsey, as the boys call this paradise of pedagogy....*" Hannon began, and then elaborated enough florid encomium to fill one side of the page, averring to the brilliant faculty, the manly athletics, the hours filled with fellowship and fun, the splendid cuisine, and so forth. When Jeff had addressed an envelope, Frosty and Shaner hoisted him out of the swivel chair and out of the suite, with Hannon following. Soon, they were in part of the basement that contained a swimming pool. The tiled walls were decorated with vignettes of nymphs chased by satyrs, a motif chosen by original builder, asbestos magnate Felix Fogelhaus, when the central portion of the Great Hall was his private summer mansion. Hannon's henchmen stripped and told Jeff to do likewise. While Hannon smoked on the tiled bench seat that ran along the wall, Frosty and Shaner dragged Jeff into the shallow end and took turns holding him underwater until his lungs nearly burst and, after repeated duckings, finally hauled him out, gasping and choking. He remained sprawled on the cold tiles when they departed, turning the lights off on their way out so it took Jeff a quarter of an hour to locate his clothing in the windowless chamber, and then feel his way along the clammy walls to the door. In the event, he missed supper.

When he got back upstairs to Two-West, he went to the room next door to his where Andelthorne and Veach lived.

"What happened to you?" Veach asked.

"I can't take it anymore," Jeff said. "The bastards tried to drown me in the pool."

"Who did that?" Andelthorne asked, lowering his *Archie and Jughead* comic book. He was the offspring of at least four generations who had never had to work for a living, with the resultant effect on his mental development.

"You know who," Jeff retorted.

"The Ancients," Veach whispered, in case the walls had ears.

"What are you going to do?" Andelthorne asked.

"I've gotta talk to Doc Stilgoe about this."

"You can't do that," Veach said. "They'll really kill you when they find out."

"No," Jeff said. "Enough is enough. Do you have any idea where Doc lives in this dump?"

Andelthorne shook his head.

"I wouldn't do that if I were you," Veach said. "You'll end up dead like Hohenhorst."

"Hohenhorst's dead?"

"Yeah."

"How do you know that?"

"He's from the same town as me down in Jersey," Veach said. "My big brother wrote me. Set himself on fire in the driveway. It was in the local paper."

"Jeezus! He committed suicide?"

"I guess."

"And your parents let you stay here?"

"His whole family's nuts," Veach said. "The mother's in the insane asylum."

"This place is an insane asylum," Jeff said, and departed the room.

He went upstairs to the third floor where the older boys had their quarters and knocked on the first door next to the stairwell.

"Come in...."

When he entered, he found the two occupants, Derek Nulley of Cos Cob, Connecticut, and Randy Geiger of Riverdale, New York, both fifteen, cooking up a batch of Chef Boyardee ravioli on a sterno stove. Nulley had been arrested for throwing snowballs filled with rocks at a commuter train. Geiger had been caught trying to buy fireworks from an undercover cop in Chinatown.

"What do you want?" Nulley asked.

"Do you guys happen to know where Doc Stilgoe actually lives?"

"Did you check his office?" Geiger said.

"He's in his office at night?"

"Yeah, since Hannon kicked him out of the tower. He sleeps there."

"Thanks," Jeff said. "Hey, you got anymore of that grub you can spare? I missed dinner."

"It'll cost you," Nulley said.

"How much?"

"Two bucks a can?"

"What, are you kidding me? It only costs thirty-nine cents in the store!"

"Then take yourself down to the store and get some," Geiger said.

Nulley cackled and licked the spoon he was stirring the stuff with.

Jeff withdrew from the room. He went down to the first floor and padded across the grand reception hall to the door with a frosted glass window that said *H.R. Stilgoe, Headmaster* in gold leaf. A light burned dimly within. He had to knock more than once. Finally, a fuzzy shape loomed behind the window and the door opened. The headmaster wore an earth-colored cardigan sweater over his usual khakis.

"What is it, child?"

"I have to talk to you, sir?"

"Come in then."

The office was spacious and nicely appointed with a wall of shelves groaning with books, framed prints of American Indian scenes by the great George Catlin and Karl Bodmer, and shadow-boxes of colorful Indian artifacts. A genuine oil painting of Arikira braves stalking buffalo by Frederic Remington hung over the fireplace. Stilgoe poked at the embers and tossed a new log on. Two leather club chairs were deployed by the hearth. The headmaster pointed to one with the poker.

"Have a seat, my boy."

Jeff slid into the chair, his shoes just barely touching the worn oriental carpet. Stilgoe lowered himself into the other with a slight arthritic groan. For an elongated moment he said nothing. Jeff glanced around the room. He noticed that a leather sofa that matched the club chairs was made up somewhat haphazardly with sheets and blankets, indicating that someone was sleeping there.

"Nothing like a nice fire on a cold autumn night, eh?" Stilgoe broke the silence. "The

Kiriwaska of the Loess Hills of Nebraska said they saw the face of the Great Spirit in every fire. I think they were onto something."

"Were they an Indian tribe?" Jeff asked.

"Yes, and a peaceful, compassionate people compared to their neighbors the Minnetaree, who were very fierce and warlike."

"That's kind of like how things are here," Jeff said.

"How's that, my boy?"

"Well, you have the kids who just want to live and let live, and the ones who pick on them."

"Is somebody picking on you?"

Jeff stared into the fire, hoping to find the face of the Great Spirit there, but it was only fire.

"I'm afraid to say."

"You needn't be afraid," the headmaster said. "I'm here."

"I was warned about being a rat."

"We don't stand for bullying at Ponsonby Hall, son."

Jeff could not help seeing that this was patently untrue. He glanced across the room at the sofa again. His stomach growled and a tumult rose in his throat.

"Do you sleep down here, sir?" Jeff asked.

Stilgoe reached for a pipe in the pocket of his cardigan sweater and poked around the bowl with a little folding tool.

"Sometimes," he said, "when I have a great deal of work to do late at night."

"They say you used to live up in the tower—"

"At times over the years I have, yes."

"—where Hannon lives now."

"Mr. Hannon is a special boy."

"Did he kill his own mother? Is that why he's here?"

Stilgoe appeared shocked at the idea at first, but then dismissed it with a chuckle as he lit his pipe. "Where did you get that notion?"

"He sort of hints at it, sir, like he wants to brag about it."

"Mr. Hannon," Stilgoe said, "is an orphan."

Jeff blinked, more than once.

"Is that what's special about him?"

"No. There's a bit more to it, but I'm not at liberty to say. The boys have their privacy, after all, their private shame and sorrow. You, for example, have done some things you're probably not proud of. Shall we talk about that? I could get your file—"

"I'd prefer not to," Jeff said. "I just wish you would tell this Hannon to lay off of us younger kids. He acts like he runs the place."

Stilgoe shifted this way and that way in his seat and re-lit his pipe and appeared to be mumbling something to himself. "I run this school," he eventually blurted out. "I am the headmaster!" He seemed to make an effort to control his emotions. "I will talk to the boy," he said.

34

"Thanks," Jeff said. "Say, do you have a telephone here I can use, by any chance? I'd like to call my parents in New York."

Stilgoe bristled visibly.

"It's out of order at the moment," he said. "A tree fell on the wire out on the highway."

"Maybe I could come back some other time after they fix it—"

Just at that moment, when Jeff was about to take the giant step into spelling out some of Hannon's turpitudes, like extorting five dollars a month from everybody, and beating up kids, and nearly drowning them in the pool, the door opened and Mrs. Dinsmoor the cook stepped in the chamber, carrying a tray with things on it.

"Ooooooff!" she said, clearly flustered. "I didn't know you had company...sir."

"Just one of the boys," Stilgoe said with another forced chuckle.

"I brought you a little snack," Mrs. Dinsmoor said. "Would you like a cookie, young sir?" She lowered the tray. On it was a plate of shortbread cookies glistening with sugar crystals. Also a thermos bottle.

"Can I have two?" Jeff said. "I missed dinner because I was busy almost getting drowned to death in the pool by somebody."

"Boys...!" Stilgoe said, shaking his head mirthfully. "Have as many as you like, son,"

Jeff took four more and stuffed them in his blazer pocket.

"There's cocoa in the thermos," Mrs. Dinsmoor said.

"Here, take the thermos with you," Stilgoe said, rising from his seat and proffering the cheerful plaid-colored bottle to Jeff.

"You two can share," Mrs. Dinsmoor said.

"He was just leaving," Stilgoe said. "Thank you for visiting, Mr. uh—"

"Greenaway," Jeff said.

"Right. Run along now," Stilgoe said. "I'll talk to so-and-so about you-know what."

"You can bring the thermos back down at breakfast," Mrs. Dinsmoor said as the headmaster steered Jeff by his shoulders out the door.

*

The next day in English class, Mr. Hamdoon took the boys of the first form on a journey into the strange world of Herman Melville's *Bartleby the Scrivener*, the short story of an elderly Wall Street Lawyer in the 1850s who hires a peculiar young man to make copies of legal documents in long-hand, this being before the invention of the typewriter. Pretty soon, the young man, Bartleby, starts refusing to work. When asked to do anything, or answer any questions about his identity and origins, Bartleby replies by saying, *"I would prefer not to...."* Something about the phrase electrified Jeff. He recalled using almost exactly the same words the night before in Doc Stilgoe's office. As the story goes on, the narrator, never named, can't get Bartleby to attend to his tasks, or leave the office after closing, or eat any food that is brought in for him.

"Mr. Herman Melville, you see," Hamdoon held forth sitting on the corner of his desk, "has been all around the vorld on a vhaling ship and has become acquainted vith ideas and people from foreign lands. This Bartleby is a personification of the Hindu concept *Moksha* from the *Vedanta*, to be liberated from all earthly desires, a state of blissful emptiness, conscious yet implacably unconcerned. The grasping, greedy man of Vall Street cannot comprehend this behavior, this attitude to the world. All right," Hamdoon clapped his stump and his hand twice to break the spell he had cast. "Ve vill discuss the conclusion tomorrow. Go forth now, boys, to the lovely lovely rigors of mathematics!"

That evening, as had become his habit in as much as possible avoiding proximity to the nauseating person of his room-mate Axel Knudsen, Jeff was hiding out in a corner of the first floor study lounge when Frosty and Shaner barged in like a couple of roughnecks entering a Wild West saloon. They vectored in on his chair in the corner, obviating any chance at escape.

"Where were you today?" Shaner said. "We miss you."

"Plus which, you're neglecting your duties," Frosty said. "Come with us."

"I would prefer not to," Jeff said, over his volume of Melville's *Piazza Tales*.

The two Ancients shared an incredulous glance and cracked up laughing.

"He'd prefer not to!" Shaner said, pointing.

"Get up!" Frosty said.

"I'd prefer not to," Jeff said.

"The temerity!" Shaner said.

"Move it!" Frosty barked.

"I'd prefer not to."

"Okay, have it your way," Shaner said.

The two quickly overwhelmed Jeff, grabbed him by his ankles, and dragged him out of the room, to the silent astonishment of the only other occupant of the study lounge, one Leslie Sorrel, third form, of Belmont, Mass., whose moderate Tourette's syndrome had been taken for obdurate rudeness in his previous school.

"Damn you, damn you, damn you, goddammit," he blurted as the others exited.

Frosty and Shaner attempted to drag Jeff up the stairs off the grand reception hall, but they gave up on the first landing, considering they had to haul him all the way to the fifth floor.

"Get up and walk, maggot," Frosty said.

"I'd prefer not to," Jeff replied.

"What's all this *I'd prefer not to* crap about?" Shaner said.

Jeff said nothing.

"Speak, maggot!"

"I'd prefer not to."

"Arrrggghhh!" Frosty cried and shoved Jeff back down the stairs supine so that he slid like a toboggan on a bumpy hill to the hall below.

The two Ancients continued upstairs without him.

Jeff lay there on the polished marble floor for a while, taking inventory of his lumps and bumps a little tearfully, and eventually limped back to Two-West-twenty-seven and his odoriferous room-mate. He'd barely crawled under the covers when the door flew open revealing the baleful silhouette of Hannon, and the two others behind him in the hallway. The harsh overhead light was flipped on.

"I hear you've been insolent," Hannon said. "Get up."

"I'd prefer not to," Jeff said.

"Hey, I was sleeping!" Knudsen said. "What's the big idea?"

"The big idea is: shut up, Stench, if you know what's good for you," Frosty said.

"C'mon, let's go Greenaway."

"I'd prefer not to."

"Who do you think you are, Bartleby the Scrivener?" Hannon said. Unlike his two cohort Ancients, Hannon had started Ponsonby in the first form and taken Hamdoon's introductory AmLit class. "I'm sure you know how he ended up, don't you?"

As a matter of fact, Jeff had not quite gotten to the last few pages of Melville's tale.

"I'd prefer not to," Jeff said.

"Okay, get him out of his rack," Hannon said.

The other two seized Jeff and extracted him from the bed.

"How'd you like to go on a little adventure?" Hannon asked.

"I'd prefer not to," Jeff said, tears spilling down his face.

"Silly me for asking," Hannon said. "Well, off we go then!"

"Hey, turn out the light!" Knudsen said, punching his pillow and flipping over to face the wall.

The Ancients dragged Jeff back downstairs, and out the rear of the great hall to the terrace, and then across the playing fields and into the woods, where they brought out their flashlights, and then down a well-worn bosky path to where the path ended, and then through a succession of glades, hollows, groves, sloughs, defiles, thickets, and uplands until the very existence of something called civilization seemed a dim dream of a long-lost homeland. At the terminus of this trek, they tied a rope around Jeff's left leg and the other end around the trunk of a scabrous hawthorn tree (*Crataegus scabrida*) with a sufficient number of complicated knots to keep Jeff occupied long enough for them to make a get-away.

"Have fun!" Hannon called from a distance, and soon even their bobbing flashlights disappeared in the murk.

A less-than-quarter moon kept darting in and out from behind clouds as though it were just another cruelly teasing adversary in Jeff's life. It took him twenty minutes to get all the knots out and free himself, and then he had no idea which direction to go in. They had dragged him away from Ponsonby dressed only in his flannel pajamas, with no shoes, and it was painful to tread on the floor of the woods with all its rocks and twigs and fallen logs. What's more, his latent fear of the dark melded with his fear of the trackless woods, along with a purely cultivated fear of supernatural monsters and creatures from outer space — often encountered in woods like these by hapless victims in the horror movies he loved — to induce a state of utter panic in Jeff, causing him to bash about this way and that way, shrieking and crying, stumbling over things and bumping into trees and boulders, until he collapsed in a heap on the forest floor in a grove of sugar maples. It was a mild October night by New Hampshire standards, just above fifty degrees, and not long after Jeff ceased bashing around in a panic, he began to shiver. Because it was autumn, and because the forest around Ponsonby Hall was of the mixed northern hardwood type, Jeff found an abundance of leaves to burrow into, and he curled up under a heap of them in a shivering ball to await the dawn, praying that the werewolves, blood-beasts, vampires, carnivorous space blobs, and other creatures of his imagination — not to mention the real-life bears and mountain lions — would fail to notice and beset him .

*

When he awoke around dawn — which is to say that sleep had actually found him for a while, despite his galloping terror — Jeff decided to get moving at once under the theory that it would at least warm him up. He had no idea where to go, but the sun was breaking low on the horizon and he figured if he moved straight toward it he would at least not go around in circles. The woods still spooked him with its ominous silence and incomprehensible vastness but he soldiered on in the new day's light and within an hour he heard the distinctive noise of cars and trucks passing nearby on a highway. He clambered up an embankment and bashed through a final obstructing honeysuckle thicket to find himself at the edge of New Hampshire State Route 118. Not ten seconds later, a beige 1952 DeSoto with a front grill of glowering chrome "teeth" came into view in the oncoming lane. Jeff stepped onto the road and began jumping up and down and waving his arms.

The car screeched to a stop some distance ahead and Jeff ran up to it, lunging for the heavy door.

"You!" cried the driver when he put his head inside. This blue-haired driver happened to be Mrs. Dinsmoor, Ponsonby Hall's very cook on her way to work from the town of Orcus at six-thirty in the morning. "What are you doing out here? Dressed like that!"

"Hannon and his goons dragged me into the woods and tied me to a tree."

"Oh, dear...."

"I've got to get out of this place. I've got to get back home before they kill me. Please, take me to the police!"

"Now, now...." Mrs. Dinsmoor said. "No need to involve them. I'm sure Doc Stilgoe will straighten—"

"I wanna go home!"

"That's just where we're going," Mrs. Dinsmoor said. "There there, now...."

Jeff bawled his eyes out all the rest of the way to Ponsonby Hall, which was roughly three and a half miles up the twisting road — though the distance he had actually traversed through the woods from his initial capture to his intersection with the road was only a mile and three quarters. At least the heater was on in the old car, and the wool upholstery had a comforting feel, and Mrs. Dinsmoor herself gave off a reassuring scent like butter. When they parked at the rear of the east wing, she led Jeff by the hand to her modest office in the school kitchen, where Irma the prep girl (a woman of forty-two, actually, of limited abilities) was already at work refreshing the perpetual pot of oatmeal.

It happened that Mrs. Dinsmoor filled a second unofficial role at Ponsonby Hall, playing school nurse as occasion required. "My my, aren't you a sight..." she said, attending to Jeff's many scrapes and scratches and bruised feet, painting them with orange mercurochrome from the kitchen first aid kit, bandaging them where necessary, and carefully sponging the dirt and mud off him.

"Can I use your phone?" Jeff said.

"Why would you want to do that?"

"To call my parents and tell them I'm going to commit suicide if they don't come up and get me out of this place."

"I'm, uh, afraid the telephone's out of service just now, dear."

"How do you know? You haven't tried it since we got here."

"Oh," Mrs. Dinsmoor said, "We received advanced notice that they would be working on the line today. They told us in no uncertain terms not to touch it. They're testing the circuits with very high voltage electricity."

"If that's true, I'll give it a try," Jeff said. "It'll save me from having to commit suicide."

"Oh, p'shaw," she said. "You run along to your quarters now and change into some decent clothes. I have to prepare the rest of today's breakfast for you little scamps. Go on now, shoo!"

Jeff left the kitchen and went directly to Doc Stilgoe's office. He knocked on the door more than once. No light burned within. In fact, the headmaster had left quite early that morning on a mysterious mission to meet a certain someone in Orcus before the mills there opened for the day-shift.

Jeff proceeded up to his room on the second floor. Axel Knudsen was already awake, pulling on his underpants. The room smelled like the rectified essence of a thousand sweaty gym socks.

"Hey, where'd you go last night?" Knudsen asked.

"Are you concerned about me?" Jeff retorted.

"I just noticed you didn't come back."

"Yeah, because Hannon and his goons tied me to a tree way out in the woods. Did you happen to report to anyone that they dragged me out of here?"

"Why would I do that? They'd come back and get me."

Jeff had just finished knotting his official scarlet Ponsonby necktie in the mirror and, in a rather deft move that surprised even himself, spun around and landed a roundhouse punch on the side of Knudsen's slightly lopsided head. The much larger boy fell back onto his bed, stupefied.

"You… hit me!" he sputtered.

"Do you ever take a goddam bath?" Jeff shouted at him.

"They don't have baths here," Knudsen said. "Only showers."

Jeff stormed out of the room and down to the very end of the hall where he pounded on Mr. Hamdoon's door.

The Master of Two West answered in a dressing gown of riotous orange paisley, made in his home village of Farrukhabad in the province of Uttar Pradesh.

"A boy calls at the master's door!" he said with his right hand and left stump pressed together as in prayer and the broad smile of someone who greets each new day, and every event in it, with a profound gratitude for being. "How can the master be of service?"

"Call the police!" Jeff said.

Hamdoon's smile vanished. He grabbed Jeff by the upper arm, yanked him inside, and kicked the door shut with his slippered foot. The room, which occupied a turreted corner of the building, was very large with a round outer wall, and was decorated with plush and vivid eastern carpets and drapes. It smelled of exotic spices, sandalwood, and aromatic resins.

"Vhat is the matter that requires the police?" he asked.

"Hannon is trying to kill me."

Hamdoon let out a sigh of grievous disappointment.

"Hannon, Hannon, Hannon...." He muttered to himself. "Oh, this boy...! Vhat has he done now?"

Jeff told Hamdoon the whole story and then some, going back to the initiation ceremony and the ensuing program of extortion, oppression, and persecution that followed it, and then his late misadventure out in the woods overnight.

"Come, sit, boy," Hamdoon said, gesturing to a pair of fat Oriental pillows beside a low table with a brass teapot on a brass tray. "Like so," Hamdoon demonstrated, sitting down cross-legged. The cushions were deployed in front of a big, arched, floor-to-ceiling window that looked out on the playing fields and the endless woods beyond, blazing with color. Hamdoon had been enjoying his morning tea there and ruminating, if not exactly meditating, on the landscape before he was interrupted. Jeff sat on the other pillow

"Do you have a phone?" he asked.

"I have no need of one," Hamdoon said. "This is my whole vorld, lovely lovely Ponsonby. See how beautiful it is!"

"It's a hell-hole if you're a kid."

"Don't say that."

"I already did, and I won't take it back. You've got to help me get out of this place."

"Hmmph," Hamdoon snorted. He refilled his brass teacup and poured a fresh one for Jeff. The tea was inky-black and loaded with sugar.

"This is vhat I propose," Hamdoon said. "I vill confab vith this... this *troubled* boy, Mr. Hannon — and, if necessary, knock sense into his silly silly head!

"He's not troubled," Jeff said, "he's evil."

"A boy cannot be evil, only ignorant."

"You're wrong about that."

"I cannot be wrong in this case. I am the Master of Two Vest. I have known hundreds of boys. I vas a boy myself once in a faraway land. I know boys. Boys can be rascals, yes, but even a bad boy can become a good boy vith patience and understanding, and perhaps a knock on the head."

"Sooner or later I'm going to get a hold of my parents and tell them what's going on here" Jeff said. "My father's an attorney. He'll sue this joint for all it's worth."

Hamdoon, sipping his tea, gagged slightly.

"My dad once sued Walter Winchell," Jeff added.

"And who is this Valter Vinchell?"

"He writes for the newspaper, and he's lying, evil sack of you-know-what, my dad said. He'll ruin this lousy place."

"You cannot do this. I cannot allow it!"

"You can't stop him," Jeff said, and got up and made for the door.

"All right!" Hamdoon cried.

"All right, what?" Jeff said, his hand on the doorknob.

"All right, I vill tell you vhat you need to know in this delicate matter."

"What do I need to know besides where is there a telephone that works around here?"

Hamdoon struggled up from his pillow and approached Jeff meekly, like a supplicant in the court of an Oriental despot. He bent so closely to Jeff's ear that his long mustache tip brushed Jeff's face and tickled him.

"Mr. Hannon is Doctor Stilgoe's son?"

"What?"

"I vill not repeat it. You heard vhat I said."

"How can that be? They don't even have the same name."

"Please, boy, sit down again and I vill explain. I cannot let you destroy lovely lovely Ponsonby Hall."

And so Jeff was induced back to the tea table overlooking the rugged gold and crimson New Hampshire scene, where Hamdoon told him that some years ago the very very lonely Doc Stilgoe had succumbed to a dalliance with one of the cleaning ladies, a woman from Orcus named Hannon, the product of which dalliance was young Mr. Hannon, who, upon the tragic early death of his mother in a car wreck, was enrolled at Ponsonby Hall and raised there through the remaining days of his childhood, and sent away to summer camps when school was not in session.

"But the matter of his origins remain a secret," Hamdoon said, "even unto himself. He has been told only that he is the offspring of an unnamed Ponsonby alumnus, now a gentleman of riches and influence, who cannot acknowledge him."

"You mean, he doesn't know that Doc is his father?" Jeff said.

"That is correct."

"Is that why Doc lets him do anything he wants around here?"

"Alas, Mr. Hannon has been led to believe he is very very special. Let us say, the headmaster has been... indulgent. Apparently to a fault. The headmaster has been to me, Khan Hamdoon of Uttar Pradesh, like unto a father, too. So I am pleading with you, young sir, do not instigate the ruin of this grand old establishment and this most excellent man. If you please, I shall contact your parents and advise them that you would thrive less indifferently at another school of equal distinction — if such a place exists."

Hamdoon added to his verbal plea a particularly piteous look of entreaty.

"What about Hannon in the meantime?" Jeff asked. "He'll come after me again, I'm sure."

"I vill beat him like a dog. And I vill inform the headmaster that something must be done about him. There it 'tis." Hamdoon added. "Now, you must svear to never disclose this confab between yourself and myself.

"Why? I didn't ask you to tell me all this?"

"Because," Hamdoon said, "I have shared it with you as a gentleman, and a gentleman is honorable vith secrets and does not divulge them."

"What if Hannon tries to kill me again?"

"It vill not happen, I promise you."

Jeff pondered the proposition.

"Okay, I'll try it your way... for now," he conditionally agreed. "Say, have you got anything to eat up here? I'm starving," he said.

"Sorry," Hamdoon offered a weak smile. "Mice, you know." He glanced at his wristwatch. "Ah! They are serving breakfast down below in five minutes. Come."

*

Jeff entered the refectory, bustling at this hour with hungry boys lining up with their trays. He received his bowl of oatmeal and his plate of bacon, scrambled eggs, toast, and carton of milk and settled into the table where Andelthorne and Veach and some of the other first form boys were chowing down. He could see Hannon and his two cronies seated across the room, being waited on by boys of the middle forms. One of them poured steaming coffee for the trio from a metal pot. Another proffered a tray of donuts. Nobody else got donuts.

51

When all the boys were served and seated, Hannon stood up and tapped on an empty drinking glass with a spoon until a hush fell over the large room.

"A little housekeeping business, Ponsenbynians," he said in his characteristic world-weary manner. "November is almost upon us, and a number of you writhing little maggots are still in arrears with your October contributions to the, uh, sinking fund. You, for instance, Mr. Lamson," he intoned, reading from a scrap of paper in his hand. "Where are you?"

Edward Lamson, 16, fifth form, of Locust Valley, Long Island, shipped off to Ponsonby for pouring Karo syrup into the gas tank of a Buick Riviera belonging to the father of a girlfriend who dumped him, stood up near the center of the room.

Jeff scoured the room to locate Mr. Hamdoon. He was over at the side, near the glass cases filled with athletic trophy cups and assorted Ponsonby sporting memorabilia. His head was down so low to the table that only the back of his saffron-colored turban was visible.

"You're five bucks short this month, Lamson. Cough it up," Hannon said with a self-satisfied smile. "Come on, get up here...."

"I would prefer not to," Lamson replied.

"What's that?" Hannon said, his smile disintegrating.

"I'd prefer not to," Lamson repeated himself.

Hannon goggled at him.

"You too, huh?" he said.

The hush in the room was so complete that Mrs. Dinsmoor and her helper, Irma, could be heard back in the kitchen discussing the upcoming chores for the day's lunch.

"I don't care what you'd prefer, Lamson," Hannon continued. "This concerns your obligations, not your miserable maggoty little preferences, hopes, and desires. I'll see you later in your lodgings, and it won't be pretty. Siddown!"

Hannon referred back to the paper in his hand.

"Mr. Warburton," he said. "Where are you?"

Curtis Warburton, 15, fourth form, of Bethesda, Maryland, consigned to Ponsonby for repeatedly calling in false alarms to the fire department (but since that time a model student and winner of the Sapir Award for foreign language studies), stood up one table over from Jeff's.

"Mr. Warburton... good gracious! I see here that you are two months short. How did that happen? Please come up and see Mr. Shane to bring your account up-to-date."

"Je préférerais ne pas."

"I didn't quite get that," said Hannon, who had chosen Spanish as his foreign language study.

"I would prefer not to," Warburton translated, rather emphatically.

This time, a murmur rumbled through the room.

"Very funny," Hannon said. "I'd prefer not to come up to your maggoty trash-can of a room later, too, but I will if I must. Better gird your loins for some rough-and-tumble, pal."

The volume of murmuring rose another increment. Frosty banged on the table with his coffee mug and the hubbub subsided a bit.

"Mr. Sorrel!" Hannon now barked. "Rise and face the Ancients!"

Leslie Sorrel, 14, who had been present in the study lounge the day Jeff was dragged out, stood up.

"Mr. Sorrel, you are chronically late and disrespectfully so, I might add," Hannon said, noticeably nervous now. And, no, we do not accept baseball cards in lieu of US currency. Step forward and pay up!"

"I would prefer not to, goddam you...." Sorrel said, suddenly gripped by a fugue of Tourette's syndrome, "and go fuck yourself, you goddam fucking piece of shit!" he concluded. And sat back down.

The refectory exploded in cheers and applause.

Frosty, Shaner, and even Hannon himself pounded on the table with their coffee mugs yelling for order, but to no avail. Soon, cries erupted from all corners of the room: "I prefer not to! I prefer not to!" And before long, the individual cries resolved into a mighty chant by all the boys: "I PREFER NOT TO!" And after a minute or so of that, all the boys in the room rushed the Ancients' table, and upended it, and set upon Hannon, Frosty, and Shaner until Mrs. Dinsmoor and Ida rushed out of the kitchen to break it up. Eventually, Mr. Hamdoon himself had to intervene to rescue the two ladies of the kitchen. And so transpired the fall of the Ancients, who were never again able to tyrannize the other boys of Ponsonby Hall. But the story does not quite end here.

*

The rebellion occurred, of course, because word of Jeff Greenaway's valor in single-handedly opposing the regime of Hannon and the Ancients had crackled like lightning through Ponsonby Hall's classrooms, corridors, and dormitory wings, inspiring and emboldening all the other Ponsonbynians to throw off the shackles of their wretched servitude. Jeff Greenaway, in other words, young as he was, became an instant hero to his schoolmates. It didn't go to his head, but in the weeks going forward it greatly altered the ambience of daily life of the school for the better and prompted a new spirit of fraternity among the students so that despite the torments of their personal histories, every one of them began to thrive far less indifferently than had been the case before.

Mr. Hamdoon kept his promise regarding Mr. Hannon, calling on him in the tower suite that very afternoon and thrashing him roundly with a rattan cane until Hannon offered him a hundred dollars cash to lay off, upon which disgusting ungentlemanly proposal Mr. Hamdoon thrashed him even more heartily, adding a number of kicks to Hannon's hindquarters with the old-fashioned English paddock boots that he had come to love back in his military days.

It marked the end not just of the Ancients, but of John C. Hannon's career at Ponsonby Hall. For as soon as Doc Stilgoe returned from his errand in the town of Orcus before lunch, he made arrangements for the boy to be enrolled in the remote and severe Ballycraggan School on the Isle of Mull off the Scottish coast, where the boys were subject not just to cold showers, but to cold baths in North Atlantic seawater, and put on short rations for any lapses in conduct, and made to take part in the harrowing ancient game of *Plunth-be-daggit*, a Viking version of field hockey played with oaken clubs in which any sort of physical contact was permissible, and even encouraged, in moving the severed head of a ewe over the goal line. It was said to toughen up even the effete alcoholic offspring of land-poor British lords.

Doc Stilgoe's secret mission in Orcus was a meeting in the parking lot of the Pompoquoddy Blanket Mill with one Gabrielle Brousseau, 19, who had informed the headmaster that she was carrying the child of a Ponsonby Hall student named Jack Hannon. The headmaster, who had close to zero living expenses of his own, came to her support, put her in a fine apartment above the Orcus National Bank, and paid for her lying-in following the birth. Then, by a strange turn events — and who can say why some things happen as they do in this world of mystery — Doc Stilgoe married the girl, who proved to be a faithful, loving, devoted, and grateful wife, quite conscious of being rescued from a life of industrial drudgery. The child she bore was a girl, whom the couple named Nebi, the Abenaki Indian name for water. Doc Stilgoe raised her as his own daughter, a family man at last. She would go on to win an Olympic silver medal in the women's 400-meter relay and later become Director of the National Museum of the American Indian in Washington, DC.

John C. ("Jack") Hannon went to work for Goldman Sachs in 1983 and rose to the position of Executive Vice-President for Ethical Investing. He was beheaded in a Madison, New Jersey, shopping mall by a deranged Jihadist in 2014.

The End

Manufactured by Amazon.ca
Acheson, AB

30237054R00037